Splashes of Fate

Nadeera Goonetilleke

Published by Nadeera Goonetilleke, 2024.

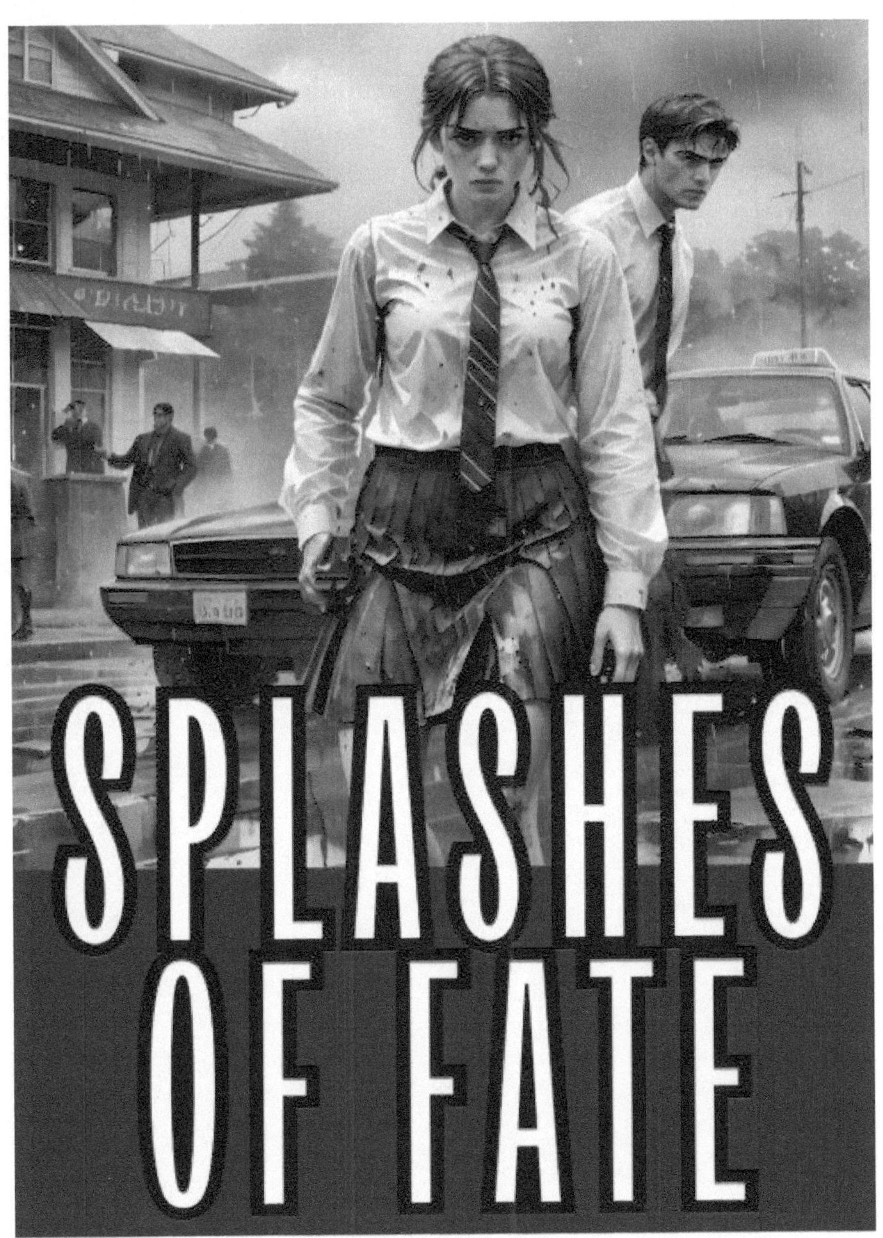

Copyright Page

Title: Splashes of Fate
Subtitle: A Journey through Love and Destiny

SPLASHES OF FATE

First edition. October 28, 2024.

Copyright © 2024 Nadeera Goonetilleke.

ISBN: 979-8227852588

Written by Nadeera Goonetilleke.

INDEX

Chapter 1: A Muddy Encounter

Eda stood under the old metal shelter of the bus halt, anxiously glancing at her watch. The rain fell in light drizzles, the sky a gloomy gray, but her spirits were high. She wore her brand-new school uniform, a pristine white blouse and a neatly pleated dark blue skirt, something she had long begged her middle-class parents to buy for her. Today was important—she was the captain of the debate team, and their school was competing against the prestigious Westwood Boys School.

Her thoughts danced between excitement and nerves. *"This is my day,"* she whispered, shifting her weight impatiently. She was 16 and full of fire, ready to take on the world—especially the boys. The bus stop was nearly empty, with just a few people passing by. Eda felt a single raindrop land softly on her cheek, and in the next moment, everything in her world shifted dramatically.

SPLASH!

A car zoomed by, sending a wave of muddy water crashing onto her, soaking her uniform from head to toe. The icy liquid clung to her clothes, and her neat appearance was now a mess of dirt and grime. Eda gasped, her breath catching in her throat before it turned into a roar of fury. Anger flooded her as she stared at her ruined uniform.

"WHAT THE HELL!" Eda screamed, storming toward the sleek, black car. She planted herself firmly in front of it, hands on her hips, eyes blazing with righteous indignation.

Inside the car, Earl Davidson, a composed bank executive with his usual calm demeanor, remained unaware of what had just happened. Deep in thought, he was still preparing himself for a tense meeting later that day. It wasn't until he spotted a small, furious figure standing in his way that he was jolted back to reality.

Earl rolled down the window, confusion flickering across his face. "Excuse me, miss, is there a problem?" he asked in a tone that was far too casual for what was coming his way.

Eda's eyes narrowed, her fists clenched at her sides. "Problem? Oh, you think this is just a 'problem'? Look at me!" She pointed down at her muddy uniform, the once-bright white now a streaked mess of brown and filth. "You've completely ruined my day, you—"

"I'm sorry, I didn't see—" Earl started, his voice still calm but slightly strained.

"Didn't see? Didn't SEE?" she interrupted, her voice rising. "Are you BLIND? Look at what you did! I have a debate today, the biggest debate of my life, and I can't show up like this!" Her voice cracked as she gestured wildly to her soaked, mud-streaked clothes. "Do you know how hard I worked for this? And now you've gone and ruined everything!"

Earl frowned slightly, taken aback by her fiery response. He had seen many outbursts before, but this girl was a force of nature. "I said I'm sorry," he repeated, a bit more firmly this time. "It wasn't intentional."

"Sorry isn't going to fix my uniform, now, is it?" Eda snapped, her eyes filled with tears of frustration as she wiped her face. "Do you even realize what this means to me? I begged my parents for this uniform, and now... now, look at me! I can't go to school like this!"

Earl ran a hand through his hair, his mind racing for a solution. She was visibly upset, and he couldn't blame her. A quick glance at his watch reminded him that he *would have* a meeting in half an hour, yet he had a feeling this situation wouldn't be resolved so easily.

"Alright, alright," he said, raising his hands in a gesture of peace. "Let me make it up to you. I'll... I'll buy you a new uniform."

Eda's eyes widened in surprise, though she quickly masked it with a scowl. "And what makes you think that's going to solve everything?" she retorted, though the idea of a fresh uniform did sound appealing. "You think you can just throw money at a problem and it'll go away?"

Earl sighed, sensing the debate wasn't over just yet. "I'm not throwing money at the problem, I'm trying to help," he replied, his voice firm but measured. "Look, I'm offering to fix this. You're clearly in a hurry, so let's not waste more time. I'll drive you to the nearest shop, get you a new uniform, and take you to school."

Eda crossed her arms, her lips pursed in a tight line. "I don't need your charity," she said, though the idea of getting to school on time without having to face the humiliation of her ruined uniform was tempting.

"But... fine," she huffed, after a long pause. "I'll accept your offer, but only because I'm late."

Earl opened the passenger door for her. "Get in. Let's get this sorted."

Reluctantly, Eda slid into the seat, still fuming but relieved. The car was spotless, smelling faintly of leather and cologne, which only made her feel more out of place in her muddy state. Earl drove in silence, sensing that any further words might ignite another argument.

They pulled up to a sizable clothing shop, and Earl quickly parked. He gestured toward the entrance. "Let's go. I'll take care of it."

Eda followed him into the store, still muttering under her breath. She picked out a fresh uniform while Earl quietly paid at the counter. As she emerged from the changing room in the crisp, clean clothes, a strange feeling settled over her—a mix of relief and, dare she admit, gratitude. But she wouldn't show it, of course. Not after what had happened.

She walked past Earl without a word, her nose slightly in the air as if she had won some invisible battle.

"Alright, let's get you to school before you're too late," Earl said, his patience wearing thin.

Eda sighed as she slipped back into the car. "Finally! I can't be late for the debate." Earl nodded in acknowledgment. She couldn't hide her excitement about having two uniforms now; it felt like a major victory for her.

Chapter 2: The Exaggerated Tale

Eda rushed through the school gates, her heart still racing from the morning's chaotic events. She had barely thanked Earl before bolting out of his car and sprinting toward the main building. The rain had slowed, but her nerves hadn't. She could already hear the chattering of students echoing through the corridors. This was her chance to spin the morning into a wild story, and she was determined to make it unforgettable.

As Eda headed toward the classroom, she noticed her friends huddled together on the playground, gossiping as usual. Chloe, her best friend and the most inquisitive of the bunch, was the first to spot her.

"There she is!" Chloe called out, waving her arms dramatically. "Eda, where have you been? We were starting to think you bailed on us for the debate!"

Eda plastered a smug grin across her face, reveling in the attention she was about to get. "Oh, you would *not* believe the morning I've had," she said, drawing out her words for effect as she approached her friends.

Sarah, always the one to catch onto Eda's dramatic flair, raised an eyebrow. "What happened? Did you fall into a puddle or something?"

Eda halted in her tracks, her eyes widening in feigned outrage. "A puddle? Oh, Sarah, darling, that would have been far too easy," she declared, tossing her hair over her shoulder as if she were about to unveil an epic tale.

No, no. I faced a real disaster. And look at me—I'm still here, aren't I? Ready to debate and wipe the floor with those Westwood boys.

Oh, come on, spill it! Chloe said, nudging her impatiently. You're dying to tell us.

Eda leaned in, her voice dropping to a conspiratorial whisper that drew her friends closer. "So, there I am at the bus stop, just minding my own business in my brand-new uniform," she started, gesturing dramatically to her impeccably pressed outfit. "And then, out of nowhere, this car zooms past and splashes muddy water all over me! I was drenched from head to toe."

What? Chloe gasped, covering her mouth with her hand. No way! Who was driving?

Eda paused to bask in the drama. "Oh, just some guy in a black car," she replied casually, as if the mere mention of it heightened the incident's significance. "He seemed like an executive, but he didn't even see me standing there!"

Sarah's eyes widened. "Are you serious? That's horrible! What did you do?"

What did I do?" Eda repeated, her voice rising. "I marched right up to him and gave him a piece of my mind, that's what! I wasn't going to let him just drive off like nothing happened.

Chloe's eyes gleamed with admiration. You? Strutting up to some stranger? Of course you did! What did he say?

Eda crossed her arms and smirked, recalling the moment in all its exaggerated glory. "Well, at first, he tried to act all apologetic, like 'Oh, I didn't see you,' blah blah blah," she said, imitating Earl's calm voice with an overly dismissive tone. "But I wasn't having any of it. I told him straight that he ruined my day, ruined my uniform, and I wasn't going to let it slide."

"And then?" Sarah asked, her eyes wide, hanging on every word.

Eda grinned triumphantly. "And *then*—get this—he actually offered to buy me a new uniform. Just like that. Like he could fix everything with money!"

Chloe gasped. "Wait, he *bought* you a new uniform?"

"Oh yes," Eda said, waving a hand as if it was no big deal. "Drove me to the nearest shop, paid for the whole thing. So now, thanks to Mr. Mud Splash, I've got *two* uniforms." She gave a self-satisfied smile, clearly pleased with how the story had unfolded.

Sarah laughed in disbelief. "Eda, only you could turn something like that into an advantage."

Chloe's eyes narrowed as she asked the question that had clearly been on her mind from the beginning. "But wait, was he... you know, *cute*?"

Eda hesitated for a moment, the question catching her off guard. She hadn't really thought about it at the time, but now, replaying the memory, she realized Earl wasn't exactly bad-looking.

With his neat, tailored suit and that air of confidence about him, he definitely wasn't the average guy she'd encounter at school.

She shrugged, trying to play it cool. "I mean... I guess he was *okay*," she said, but Chloe saw right through her.

"*Okay?*" Chloe repeated, crossing her arms and raising an eyebrow. "Come on, Eda. Spill."

Eda rolled her eyes dramatically but couldn't help the small smile creeping onto her face. "Fine. He was... decent-looking, alright? Tall, smart-looking, whatever."

Chloe gasped once more, this time with excitement. "I knew it! A handsome guy buys you a uniform and gives you a ride to school? Eda, this is straight out of a movie!"

Sarah laughed. "Exactly! You know, the scene where the nice guy and the headstrong girl argue and then end up falling for each other!"

Eda snorted, waving her hand dismissively. "Please. The guy was a total bore. He barely said anything after I yelled at him. Just did what I told him to. Definitely not my type."

Chloe giggled. Not your type? You mean the kind who drives a luxury car, buys you new clothes, and gives you lifts to school?

Eda sighed in exasperation. I'm serious! He's just another guy who thinks he can fix everything with money.

Sarah smirked. But you let him, didn't you?

Eda paused, her defiance wavering for a second. "Well, I wasn't about to walk into school looking like a swamp creature, was I?"

The group burst into laughter, and even Eda found it hard to hide her smile. Yet, beneath the surface, she felt an unusual flutter in her stomach at the thought of Mr. Mud Splash—the way he had calmly dealt with her outburst, despite her having unleashed her full fury on him.

Chloe nudged her again. "So, are you going to see him again? Maybe find another excuse for him to rescue you?"

"Don't be silly," Eda retorted, "he's probably already forgotten all about it."

"Oh, I highly doubt that," Sarah replied, shaking her head. "A girl like you? He definitely couldn't just forget."

"Ugh, you're all impossible," Eda groaned, rolling her eyes but unable to suppress the small smirk creeping onto her lips. "Now, can we please focus on the debate? We have boys to defeat."

As the bell rang, marking the beginning of their day, Eda found herself pondering whether Chloe and Sarah were onto something. There was an undeniable echo of that morning still lingering in her thoughts, and despite her confident exterior, she couldn't fully shake the memory of Mr. Mud Splash and the surprising twist her day had taken.

Chapter 3: Earl's Contemplation

Earl leaned back in the driver's seat, gripping the steering wheel tighter than usual as he maneuvered through the city streets. The morning drizzle had faded, but his thoughts were still stormy, swirling around the unexpected encounter that had so dramatically disrupted his peaceful day. As he drove toward the bank, his mind wandered back to the scene at the bus stop, where the fiery girl had stood her ground, drenched in muddy water yet unflinchingly bold.

He had left home that morning expecting nothing more than a typical day—just another morning meeting at the bank followed by a usual series of tasks. Earl was used to this life: predictable, orderly, filled with the same conversations and familiar faces. But that morning had turned out to be anything but ordinary.

Earl sighed, his thoughts playing on repeat. "How unpredictable our lives are," he mused. "You leave home expecting one thing, and an hour later, you're facing a situation you couldn't have imagined."

He shook his head slightly, struggling to make sense of it all. Earl had always taken pride in his calm demeanor, someone who rarely lost control. Yet this girl—this brat—had completely caught him off guard. Her furious, indignant expression was still fresh in his mind. She hadn't hesitated for an instant; there was no fear, no doubt, and no shame in her eyes.

"What a clever, chatty little brat," he muttered under his breath, torn between amusement and exasperation. "She could've approached the whole situation differently, but no, she acted as if the world owed her something."

Earl could still hear her sharp voice, ringing with indignation as she shouted at him. She hadn't held back, not even when he offered her a solution. There was no gratitude in her tone when he suggested buying her a new uniform, no hint of appreciation when he drove her to the store and paid for it. She had been nothing but a whirlwind of complaints and demands.

"She could have spoken to me more politely," Earl continued, his thoughts turning critical. "Maybe asked nicely instead of shouting like that. Where was her sense of respect? And what if someone had recognized me? What if a colleague or a client had seen me standing there, being berated by some schoolgirl? That would have been a blow to my reputation."

The thought of his status, the carefully cultivated image he had worked so hard to maintain, nagged at him. Earl was known for being level-headed, respectful, and professional, especially in his role as a bank executive. Yet there he was, being penalized by a teenager in front of passing pedestrians and vehicles. He winced at the mere memory of the embarrassment.

But then, as the traffic light turned red and he came to a stop, his mind shifted again. What if the roles had been reversed? What if it had been *him* at the bus stop, splashed with muddy water by some inattentive driver?

"I suppose," he thought reluctantly, "I would've been just as furious. Maybe worse. In fact, I might have yelled even louder than she did." He chuckled at the thought, realizing that, in her shoes, he might have reacted just as passionately. "I guess she had every right to be upset."

The girl's fierce determination left a peculiar impression on him. While her behavior had been confrontational, even rude, there was something undeniable about her ability to stand her ground. Soaking wet and humiliated, she still managed to display unwavering confidence without revealing a hint of vulnerability.

"Not many people have that kind of audacity these days," he reflected. "Especially not someone her age."

The more he thought about it, the more he realized that her boldness was something to be admired, even if it had put him on the defensive. She had demanded fairness, demanded that he fix his mistake, and she hadn't cowered under the weight of his authority or the fact that he was clearly older and more established. She had been fearless.

Earl sighed as the light turned green, resuming his drive to the bank. "Still," he grumbled to himself, "she could have expressed a bit more gratitude. A simple 'thank you' wouldn't have killed her."

But as the thoughts bounced around in his mind, he couldn't shake the feeling that the incident had been a wake-up call. It was true—he had been careless, distracted by his own thoughts, and it had led to this whole mess. He made a mental note to be more cautious from now on, to pay full attention to the road while driving, no matter how preoccupied he might be.

Lesson learned, he thought.Keep your focus sharp. You never know what's going to happen, or who you're going to cross paths with."

As the bank came into view, Earl straightened in his seat and took a deep breath. He had made it just in time for the meeting, but the events of the morning still lingered in his mind. He parked the car, adjusted his tie, and tried to clear his thoughts. He had work to do—there was no room for distractions.

Yet, as he stepped out of the car and walked toward the bank's entrance, the image of the defiant schoolgirl lingered, as if some part of him couldn't quite leave that moment behind.

He entered the building, greeted by the familiar sights and sounds of the bank: the clacking of keyboards, the low hum of conversation, the occasional ringing of phones. This was his world, the one he understood, where everything was orderly and in control. And yet, as he took his seat in the conference room, preparing for the meeting, his thoughts drifted back to her.

Her voice, filled with fierce determination, and the way she had seized control of the situation echoed in his mind, leaving him to wonder if their paths would intersect once more.

For now, he set those thoughts aside, but deep down, he realized that the morning had left behind more than just muddy water.

Chapter 4: The Debate Showdown

The auditorium was packed with students and teachers who had managed to sneak in. The excitement was palpable, the air filled with a mix of anticipation and tension. The debate between Eda's Redwood High School and the renowned Westwood Boys School had been the talk of the week, and now it was finally about to unfold. Eda, in her fresh new uniform (courtesy of Mr. Mud Splash, though she would never admit it), sat with her team, scanning the crowd while mentally preparing her arguments.

The topic of the debate had been chosen carefully:

"Is Artificial Intelligence a Threat to the Future of Human Jobs?"

It was a hot issue, one that would not only test the debaters' wits but also reflect the anxieties of a rapidly evolving world.

The boys' team, led by Cedrick—a confident and sharp thinker renowned for his calm yet incisive remarks—had already established themselves as tough opponents. The earlier rounds had seen both teams evenly matched, scoring equally in key areas such as clarity, content, rebuttal, and public speaking skills. Now, it all boiled down to the final round, where the captains would go head-to-head.

As the moderator called for the final round, a hush fell over the audience. Eda and Cedrick stepped forward, taking their positions at the podiums. Eda's heart raced, but she hid it behind her trademark confident smile. She knew this was it—this was the moment that would define her.

The moderator gave a brief introduction. "The final argument will be between the captains. The topic: *Artificial Intelligence – Is it a curse or a blessing for the future of human employment?* Each captain will have three minutes to present their case, followed by a rebuttal. The winner will be decided based on their argument's depth, relevance, and persuasiveness."

Cedrick was first.

Cedrick adjusted his tie, standing tall. His voice was calm, but every word carried weight. "Ladies and gentlemen, we are living in an age of unprecedented technological advancement. Artificial Intelligence is revolutionizing industries, streamlining processes, and, yes, replacing some human jobs. But let me ask you this: should we fear progress? Should we hold back innovation because we're afraid of change?"

He paused, making sure the weight of his words sank in.

"AI is not the enemy. It's a tool—one that, if used wisely, can lead to new opportunities. The rise of automation might reduce some jobs, but it will also create new ones. Just as the Industrial Revolution once did, AI is pushing us forward. The key is adaptation. The jobs of the future might not look like the jobs of today, but they will still be there. It's up to us to prepare for them, to embrace the change rather than fear it."

Cedrick looked directly at Eda as he concluded. Yes, AI will change the job market, but it's not a threat. It's a challenge, one we can overcome with the right mindset.

The audience murmured in approval. Cedrick's argument was strong—measured, balanced, and rational.

Eda stepped forward, her eyes blazing with intensity. She had heard everything Cedrick said, but she was ready to take the debate to a whole new level.

"Ladies and gentlemen," she started, her voice firm and resolute, "what Cedrick said may sound comforting, but let's consider the facts. AI is more than just a challenge; it's an existential crisis impacting millions of workers worldwide."

She took a deep breath and continued. "We're not talking about minor adjustments here. We're talking about entire industries being wiped out—truck drivers, factory workers, retail employees, even journalists. AI doesn't just change jobs; it *eliminates* them. And it doesn't create nearly enough new ones to make up for that loss. So tell me, what happens to the people who lose their livelihoods? What happens to the families that rely on those jobs?"

Her voice grew sharper. "We talk about embracing change, but are we prepared for the consequences? Not everyone can simply 'adapt' as easily as we like to pretend. The people most affected by AI aren't the ones with high-level tech skills—they're the ones with jobs that don't require advanced degrees. These are the people who are being left behind, while the gap between the rich and the poor continues to grow."

Eda paused, letting her words sink in. She saw the audience shifting in their seats, some nodding, others looking uncertain.

"And what about ethics?" she pressed on. "AI isn't just replacing jobs—it's replacing humans. Algorithms deciding who gets hired, who gets fired, who qualifies for a loan? Is that the kind of future we want? Where a machine—without empathy, without understanding—decides your fate?"

Cedrick shifted in his stance, but Eda wasn't finished yet.

"AI certainly has its advantages," she acknowledged. "It can achieve remarkable advancements in healthcare, education, and science. However, we must recognize the potential costs. We need to regulate and manage it, and above all, make sure it serves all of humanity—not just a handful of tech elites. If we fall short, we risk a future where millions are unemployed, their lives controlled by machines. That's not progress; it's a dystopia.

Eda stepped back, her eyes locked on Cedrick's. The room was silent, everyone on the edge of their seats. Even the judges seemed to be holding their breath.

Cedrick quickly returned to the podium for his rebuttal, his calm demeanor intact but with a slight edge in his voice. "Eda makes some excellent points, but let's not forget that history has always shown us one thing: technology disrupts, but it also rebuilds. The automobile replaced the horse-drawn carriage, and millions of jobs were created in manufacturing, design, and infrastructure. AI will do the same. Yes, some jobs will be lost, but the future is about re-skilling, retraining, and embracing new industries."

He took a step forward, trying to regain control of the argument. "Instead of fearing AI, we need to focus on how we can use it to our advantage, how we can ensure that every person has the opportunity to thrive in this new economy. That's where our energy should be directed—toward solutions, not fear-mongering."

Eda smiled slightly, ready to deliver her final blow. She stepped up one last time, her voice calm but full of power.

"You're right, Cedrick. We should focus on solutions. But we can't ignore the fact that AI isn't just a neutral force—it's shaped by those who create it. And right now, the people shaping AI aren't thinking about truck drivers, or factory workers, or the millions of people who will lose their jobs. They're thinking about profits. They're thinking about efficiency. And they're leaving humanity behind in the process."

She looked around the room, her gaze sweeping over the audience.

"We can't afford to be naive. We must face this issue directly, with honesty and courage. AI is not merely a tool—it's a force. And with great power comes great responsibility. It's our duty to ensure that this power is wielded for the benefit of everyone, not just a select few."

The room erupted in applause, the intensity of Eda's final argument resonating deeply with the audience and the judges. Cedrick stood quietly, acknowledging the strength of his opponent's points.

As the judges gathered to make their decision, it became clear that while both captains had delivered compelling arguments, Eda's passion, intelligence, and unflinching bravery had given her the edge.

When the final announcement came, it was no surprise: Eda's team had won the debate.

With a victorious smile, Eda turned to her teammates, basking in the triumph, but more than that—knowing she had made a difference in how people viewed the world's most pressing issue.

Chapter 5: The Homecoming

Eda rushed through the front door, her excitement barely contained as she threw her school bag onto the nearest chair. She kicked off her shoes, her heart still racing from the day's events.

"Mom! Mom!" Eda called out, her voice bubbling with triumph. "We won! Our team beat the boys! Hooray!"

In the kitchen, Eda's mother sat at the table, her gaze glued to the newspaper. Without glancing up, she raised her hand in a silent gesture for Eda to keep her voice down. 'Shhh... your brother is sleeping,' she murmured, casting a glance toward the living room where Eda's four-year-old brother was curled up on the couch, sound asleep. A warm smile spread across her face. 'Congratulations, dear. Your dad will be thrilled to hear this.

Eda, her energy too high to be subdued, bounced over to the table, practically beaming. "Yes, Mom, he's the one who helped me with so many valuable points! Oh, you should've been there—everyone was so quiet during the final round. They couldn't believe it! It'll be a day I'll never forget!"

Her mother chuckled softly, setting her newspaper aside. "I'm sure it will be, darling. You always have a way of making an impression. She got up and began organizing the dishes for lunch. "Now go wash up and enjoy your meal. You must be staving after such a big victory!

Eda rushed to take a quick shower, her mind still buzzing with thoughts of the debate and the audience's reactions. Once she had freshened up, she returned to the kitchen and settled down, eager to share every dramatic detail of the day's events.

As her mother served her rice and curry, Eda began with a deep breath. "So, Mom, you won't believe what happened this morning!"

Her mother raised an eyebrow, intrigued. "Oh? I thought the debate was the big event today."

Eda shook her head, leaning forward as though about to share a great secret. "No, no, no, it started before the debate! I was waiting at the bus halt, you know, wearing my brand-new uniform and feeling all proud and ready. And then—guess what—this black car came speeding by and *splashed* muddy water all over me!" She gestured wildly, her voice filled with exaggerated horror. "My whole uniform was ruined, Mom! I was *furious*."

Her mother covered her mouth with her hand, eyes wide in amusement. "Oh dear, that sounds dreadful! What did you do?"

Eda beamed, relishing her mother's reaction. "I definitely didn't stand there like some helpless girl! I dashed right in front of the car and blocked its path." She paused for effect, her excitement building. "I wouldn't let him move an inch until he got out and faced me. He looked like an executive from some big company."

Her mother shot her a knowing smile. So, what did this guy have to say about splashing you?

Eda puffed out her chest with pride. "Oh, he was completely taken aback! I gave him an earful and told him he had to fix this mess. And you know what? He bought me a brand-new uniform! We went to the shop, and I picked out the nicest one. Now I have two brand-new uniforms!"

Her mother raised an eyebrow, impressed but not entirely convinced. "Well, that was kind of him. But you didn't... thank him for going out of his way, did you?"

Eda's smile faded slightly as she shrugged. "Why should I thank him? He *had* to buy me a new uniform. It's the least he could do after ruining my morning! That's the only way to pacify me after what he did."

Her mother gave her a long, measured look, her lips curving into a faint smile. "Eda, I think you might have been a bit too much."

Eda frowned. "Too much? How?"

Her mother sat down across from her, leaning forward. "I understand you were upset—rightfully so—but not everyone would have handled it as well as he did. Instead of ignoring you or driving off, he listened and made things right. You have to admit, that was decent of him. Not everyone would go that far to help a stranger, let alone buy a whole new uniform."

Eda shifted uncomfortably in her seat, not used to being on the receiving end of such comments. "Yeah, but... he made the mess in the first place!"

Her mother's expression softened. "True, but sometimes it's important to show gratitude when someone goes out of their way, even if they caused the problem. A little 'thank you' would've been nice."

Eda crossed her arms, still stubborn. "Well, he didn't seem to expect it."

Her mother chuckled gently, shaking her head. "He probably didn't, but it wouldn't have hurt to express a bit of gratitude. It's always smart to leave a good impression."

Eda rolled her eyes, though a small smile tugged at her lips. "Alright, alright. Maybe next time I'll think about saying thank you if someone goes out of their way to help me."

Her mother smiled warmly. Exactly. Being courteous is important. If he had ignored you and driven away, you wouldn't have had the opportunity to play out all that drama. Not everyone is on his level, so always think before you speak. You're a bright, brave girl, and I'm so proud of you for standing up for yourself. Just remember that kindness, understanding, and gratitude can go a long way, too.

Eda nodded thoughtfully, allowing her mother's words to sink in. Perhaps Mom was right—after all, not everyone would have gone out of their way like Mr. Mud Splash had. May be I could have been gracious enough to offer a simple "thank you" as a courtesy, but my pride and anger had held me back.

But then again, she thought with a grin, she did end up with two new uniforms from the whole ordeal.

Chapter 6: A Familiar Face

The waiting area of Dr. Fernando's clinic was bustling, filled with people shifting in their seats, coughing, and checking their phones. Eda sat beside her mother, fidgeting impatiently while her little brother lay limply in her mother's lap, his face flushed with fever. The long wait had tested Eda's patience to its limits.

"Mom, how much longer do we have to wait?" Eda muttered, tapping her foot against the floor.

Her mother glanced at the number display on the wall, which had stubbornly remained stuck at 34 for what felt like ages. "We're number 45, Eda. We still have some time. Just be patient."

Eda groaned dramatically and leaned back in her chair. "How can I be patient when people are taking forever inside the doctor's office? What are they doing in there, writing novels?"

Her mother chuckled softly. "We're all waiting for the same thing, dear. Just relax. Your brother needs this."

Just then, the door to the doctor's office creaked open, and a woman stepped out, assisted by her son. Eda, already on edge, prepared to glare at whoever had monopolized the doctor's time. But when her gaze fell on the young man helping his mother, her eyes widened in disbelief.

It was him—Mr. Mud Splash.

She poked her mother lightly with her finger, still staring at the man as he guided his mother toward the medicine counter. "Mom! Look! That's him!"

Her mother, startled by the jab, glanced up from her lap. "Who? What are you talking about?"

Eda nodded toward the young man. "That guy over there with his mom. He's the one who bought me the uniform!"

Her mother squinted at the pair. Oh, really? She said, a teasing lilt in her voice. He seems like a kind guy, helping his mother. Why don't you go over and give him your belated thanks?

Eda's eyes widened as if her mother had suggested something completely absurd. "Aiyo, Mom, what are you saying? I don't even know his name! Who knows if he even remembers me? He's probably forgotten the whole thing by now."

Her mother smirked. "Forgotten? After the way you shouted at him? I'm sure your furious face is etched in his memory."

Eda couldn't help but laugh, rolling her eyes at her mother's teasing. "Well, I did give him a piece of my mind, didn't I?"

As they shared a chuckle, Earl, waiting at the medicine counter, casually turned his head toward the sound of their laughter. His eyes swept across the room until they landed on Eda and her mother. For a moment, he didn't register who she was, but after a few seconds, his memory clicked. Oh no... It's her. The uniform girl.

He almost chuckled to himself but decided to ignore it, pretending not to see them. Yet, before he could turn away completely, he felt a gentle tap on his shoulder. Turning around, he saw Eda standing there, her cheeks slightly flushed, but her usual boldness intact.

"Uh... excuse me, Mr.—" Eda started, but suddenly her mind went blank. She opted for the name she had been using all along. "Mr. Mud Splash?"

Earl raised an eyebrow, suppressing a grin. "Mr. Mud Splash?" he echoed, clearly amused.

Eda offered an awkward smile. "Yeah, I thought it was fitting. Anyway, I wanted to say... I'm sorry for yelling at you that day."

Earl tilted his head, a playful smirk forming at the corners of his mouth. "Oh? So you've had a change of heart?"

Eda nodded, shifting her weight from one foot to the other. "Well, my mom suggested I should've thanked you. So, um, thanks for the uniform. I guess I was just... a bit too angry at the time."

Earl's smile broadened. "A little? I'd say it was more like you were ready to stage a protest. But I understand."

She laughed, her shoulders relaxing. "Yeah, maybe. So... I guess I should know your actual name now. I've been calling you Mr. Mud Splash in my head."

Earl, he said with a friendly grin, Earl Davidson. He was careful not to share too much about his workplace. "And you?"

"I'm Eda," she replied, curiosity lighting up her eyes. "Eda Fernandez. Do you work around here? Is it for a company?" Earl nodded, knowing her questions were to be expected. "Yes, I work at a bank in the city."

"That's my mom over there," she continued, gesturing toward her mother. "We're here to pick up medicine for my little brother. He's got a fever, poor guy. It's been a full day for me—first, I nailed a big debate at school, and now we're here, stuck waiting in this clinic. But you know what? I—"

Earl chuckled as Eda's words poured out like a fast-moving train, each one racing after the next. Before he could respond, his mother turned to see who had captured her son's attention. She glanced Eda over from head to toe, clearly curious about the girl who seemed to be keeping him so entertained.

Eda caught the woman's gaze and offered a polite nod. "Hello, Auntie!" she said warmly, then turned back to Earl with an eager smile. "Oh, and which bank did you say you work at?"

Earl raised an amused eyebrow. Oh? Planning to come over and stir up trouble there too?

Eda laughed and waved her hand. No, nothing like that! I'm just curious. You know, in case I ever need a loan or something.

Earl shook his head, still smiling. "Alright, I'll make sure to notify you if we ever have a special offer for debate captains with a flair for stirring things up."

Touché! Eda grinned, clearly enjoying the playful exchange.

Earl purposely avoided mentioning the bank's name; he valued his professionalism and wasn't about to compromise his dignity by entertaining schoolgirls there. He had his principles and was firm in upholding them.

Her mother, observing them from her seat, smiled knowingly. She understood her daughter well; despite Eda's bubbly, impulsive nature, she had a sensitivity to others' feelings. Yet this was unusual—Eda rarely showed so much interest in a stranger, especially one she'd almost chased down in the street.

Chapter 7: The Unexpected Encounter

The next day at school, Eda practically bounced into the classroom, her eyes sparkling with excitement. She tossed her bag onto her desk, turned to her friends, and announced, "Girls, I've got news!"

Instantly, her friends crowded around, eyes wide with curiosity. "Spill it!" one of them demanded, grinning.

Eda smirked, savoring the moment. "So yesterday, we went to the doctor because my little brother was sick…"

"Wait a minute!" Sarah interrupted, her face lighting up. You're not saying the doctor was dreamy, and you were captivating him with your endless stories, are you?

Eda rolled her eyes, a grin spreading across her face. "Oh, please, not even close! Guess who strolled out of the doctor's office? Mr. Mud Splash himself—with his mom!"

The girls burst into laughter. "Mr. Mud Splash? Who even is that?" Chloe giggled, wiping away a tear.

"He's the one who bought me the uniform on debating day!" Eda said, struggling to keep a straight face. Chloe squealed, "You have to tell us everything!"

With dramatic gestures and exaggerated pauses, Eda dove into the tale, making her friends laugh harder with every word. Finally, Sarah had an idea. "Why don't we go surprise him at his bank after school?"

Eda's eyes gleamed mischievously. "I'm in! Only problem… I don't know which bank he works at."

Sarah rolled her eyes. "Some detective you are! He gave you a free uniform, and you didn't even get any info on him?"

Eda shrugged. "I'm sure he's at a bank somewhere in the city. We'll just go on a little 'bank tour' until we find him!"

The girls broke into fits of giggles, then agreed, "Alright, it's a mission. Let's go find your 'Mr. Mud Splash.'"

Wednesday after school, the "mission" was on! They darted from one bank to the next, asking for "Earl Davidson." Each time, they got blank stares and shook heads. Just as they were about to give up, Sarah spotted one last bank on the third floor of a shopping center. "One more shot, girls!"

They marched up, and Eda asked the security guard, "Is there an Earl Davidson here?"

The guard raised an eyebrow, but with a knowing smile, he replied, "Mr. Davidson just got back. May I tell him who's here?"

"Just say three students from the nearby school," Eda said, her voice trembling with excitement.

The security officer entered Earl's office and announced, "Sir, there are three school girls here to see you."

"Me?" Earl raised an eyebrow. "School girls? They're probably here to request a sponsorship for their school event. Alright, send them in."

As the guard returned and led them to Earl's office, the girls exchanged glances, stifling giggles. Earl looked up, momentarily startled as his eyes landed on Eda, then quickly regained his composure and gestured smoothly, "Please, have a seat."

Sarah spoke up first, bold as ever. "Actually, we're here to open savings accounts."

"Savings accounts?" Earl asked, clearly amused.

"Yes!" Sarah said with utmost seriousness. "Our teacher told us how important it is to start saving young, so here we are."

Earl chuckled, raising an eyebrow. Very responsible. You'll find the forms at the counter.

But Eda jumped in, actually, we want to know about any special student perks. Surely you have something interesting for students?

With a smile, Earl rubbed his temples. "Special perks, hmm? Alright, I'll fill you in. But first—would you like some refreshments?"

The girls shared embarrassed smiles but nodded eagerly. Earl called his assistant to bring some soft drinks, and as they sipped, he went over the benefits of youth accounts. Chloe leaned over and nudged Eda, whispering, go on, and ask for his number 'for more details.

Trying not to laugh, Eda looked up and said, In case we have extra questions...could we have your number?

Catching on, Earl grinned. "You can reach out to Doreen, our youth account specialist. She'll be happy to answer any questions. He handed over Doreen's contact card instead.

As they left the bank, Chloe sighed, well, that didn't go exactly as planned.

Eda shrugged, a mischievous smile lighting up her face, even as a hint of disappointment tugged at her heart. Who cares? We achieved our goal—we found him! With that, the girls erupted into laughter, their joyful sounds filling the air as they strolled home, their spirits lifted by the day's adventure.

Chapter 8: Reflections

Eda walked home with a heavy heart, replaying the events of the day over and over. As the sun set and cast a warm glow on her neighborhood, she felt a strange mixture of embarrassment, regret, and frustration. Earl's look of amused patience lingered in her mind, and she couldn't shake the feeling that her presence had only caused him trouble. She'd imagined herself as bold, standing up to him that first day, but now she wondered if she'd simply come across as an impulsive schoolgirl, the kind he might find amusing but far from remarkable.

She sighed, anticipating the teasing that awaited her at school. Her friends would turn it into a joke, giggling and poking fun at the idea that Earl might have a crush on her—or worse, reminding her that he didn't. Their casual mockery grated on her. Eda wasn't interested in flirting or romance, but she also wasn't keen on feeling like a silly child, especially not in Earl's eyes. Her friends might find her antics funny, but Eda wasn't laughing.

She had always been someone who sought victory, not over others but over herself. In her mind, success meant proving her worth and showing she could stand her ground. But today, she felt more like a girl scrambling to impress than the confident, driven person she hoped to be.

Earl likely saw her as just another mischievous teenager, and that stung. He was, after all, an adult—a respectable, composed man in his mid-twenties. She was only sixteen. The idea that he viewed her as little more than a school girl stung her pride. Eda wanted to set the record straight, to explain that she hadn't come alone just to chase after him. She wanted him to know her friends had been the ones pushing her, half-jokingly, to seek him out again after that memorable first encounter. Perhaps, if he understood that, he'd see her differently. But how could she explain all this when he hadn't even given her his number?

Just then, an idea flickered to life in her mind. She recalled having Doreen's card, which could provide her with the details she needed.

Without hesitating, she grabbed her phone and dialed, her fingers trembling slightly as she anticipated the call connecting.

Hello? Doreen's voice sounded on the other end, polite but slightly puzzled.

Hi, Doreen, Eda said, trying to sound casual. It's Eda. A friend of Earl's.

Oh, hello, Eda, Doreen responded, her voice warm but cautious.

Actually, Earl gave me his visiting card a while back, but I seem to have misplaced it, Eda continued. I was wondering—would you mind sharing his number with me?

A pause stretched between them, and Eda held her breath, wondering if her request was too forward.

Just a moment, dear, Doreen replied kindly. Eda heard the muffled sounds of movement, and then, after a few seconds, Doreen returned with Earl's number.

Thank you so much, Doreen, Eda said, trying to mask the relief in her voice.

As she hung up, a new resolve stirred in her. She would talk to Earl, not to chase a fantasy but to clear the air, to show that she was more than what he might have thought.

Eda took a deep breath as she waited for the call to connect, rehearsing her lines in her head. The phone rang twice before Earl's voice came through, warm and slightly surprised.

Hello? Earl answered, a hint of curiosity in his tone.

Hi, Earl! It's Eda, she said, trying to keep her voice steady. I hope I'm not disturbing you?

Eda! No, not at all. What's up? His friendly tone eased some of her nerves.

Well, I wanted to apologize for reaching out like this, she began, carefully choosing her words. It's a bit unexpected, I know. But my friends have been... pushing me to talk to you after that whole uniform incident. She chuckled lightly to make it sound casual.

Oh, I see! Earl said, laughter ringing through his voice. Your friends really know how to motivate, don't they? By the way, how did you manage to get my number?"

Eda smiled, anticipating his question. "Well, I got it from your bank," she replied casually, intentionally avoiding mentioning Doreen's name.

Earl paused, his expression shifting slightly. You know, typically bank staff won't give out our mobile numbers without our permission. I have a feeling you got it from Doreen.

Eda chose not to respond, letting the silence linger for a moment.

Earl, I just wanted to clarify that it's really their eagerness, not mine. I don't want you to get the wrong idea and think I'm, like, really interested or anything.

Of course, he replied, amusement dancing in his voice. Just a friendly check-in, then?

Exactly! Eda said quickly, feeling a surge of relief. I just thought it would be nice to clear the air. I really didn't mean to come off as some sort of eager fan or anything. Just a couple of school girls, you know?

Earl chuckled, clearly enjoying the banter. I appreciate the honesty. Honestly, I didn't think much of it. Your friends are amusing, though. They certainly have a way of pushing things.

Yeah... they think they're helping, Eda replied with a light laugh. But sometimes it feels like they're trying to set me up for something I didn't even sign up for!

Hey, no harm done, Earl said, his tone reassuring. I promise, I didn't take it seriously. Just a little friendly interaction, right?

Exactly! Just a casual chat, Eda reiterated, feeling more relaxed. Anyway, I didn't mean to take up too much of your time. Just wanted to say hi and clear the air.

It was nice hearing from you, Eda. Really, "Earl said, a hint of warmth in his voice. You've got a good head on your shoulders.

Thanks, Earl! That means a lot. Anyway, I'll let you get back to whatever you were doing. Have a great day!"

Thanks, you too!

Eda grinned, feeling a mix of triumph and relief

Bye, Earl!

Bye, Eda!

As the call ended, she put down her phone, feeling a sense of accomplishment. She had managed to navigate the conversation with wit and charm, leaving things on a positive note.

Chapter 9: Moments of Surprise

A few months had gone by, and the excitement and enthusiasm for Earl had gradually faded from Eda's thoughts. She threw herself into her studies and outdoor activities, spending much of her after-school hours at sports practices.

On Saturday morning, Eda's mom emerged from the kitchen and said, Eda, honey, could you help me out? Your Brother Shane's school admission is next week, and I need you to pick up some essentials his teacher requested. Your dad is buried in work, so I'm counting on you. With a warm smile, she handed Eda a few dollar bills. Just make sure you don't go overboard with anything fancy, alright? We need to stay within our budget.

Eda nodded, a slight pang of awareness hitting her as she tucked the cash into her purpose. She was too aware of how diligently her mom managed the household finances on her dad's salary. A renewed sense of determination washed over her—*one day, I'll study hard, secure a good job, and help my family ease their financial burden.* After a quick shower, she slipped into her favorite denim and a casual pink t-shirt, gearing up to navigate the bustling market of the town.

She took the road bus into town and got off near a well-known bookshop, carefully going through her mom's list while she browsed the shelves. She remembered every word her mom had said about staying within budget, resisting the urge to pick the more expensive, attractive notebooks.

As she grabbed the last item on her list, a burst of laughter from behind made her pause. She turned, and her heart skipped a beat—it was Earl, laughing with a girl around his age. The girl had a warm, easygoing smile that seemed to match Earl's energy effortlessly. The sight hit Eda harder than she expected. She had brushed off her playful chases after Earl, telling herself it was all just a bit of fun. But now, seeing him so at ease with someone else, she felt a pang she couldn't quite ignore. Taking a deep breath, she steadied herself. *Why do I feel like this?* she thought. *It's not as if he's my boyfriend or anything.* With a renewed sense of resolve, she decided to walk over and say hello—she wasn't about to let him think she was fazed.

After finishing up her shopping, she handed her items to the cashier, paid quickly, and took her bag with a confident stride. Approaching them, she called out, "Hi, Earl!

Both Earl and the girl turned, and Earl's face shifted from surprise to a warm smile of recognition. His eyes sparkled with a playful blend of amusement and curiosity as he said, Hey, Eda! How've you been? It's been a while you were quiet.

Eda smirked, crossing her arms. "Oh, you know... just keeping busy with school, sports, and a few other things. Thought I'd swing by to help my mom with some errands."

She launched into a lively rundown of her recent school events and activities, animatedly recounting her sports meet and latest achievements like an express train, hardly giving Earl a chance to breathe. The girl beside him watched with a smile, clearly amused by Eda's boundless energy.

You must be quite a character," the girl said with a friendly laugh, glancing at Earl. Earl, you should invite her to join us for a coffee. She's fun!

Earl nodded with a grin. You know, that's actually a great idea. How about it, Eda? Care for a coffee?

Eda's grin widened. "Sure, why not?"

She joined them as they headed toward a cozy café nearby. Inside, the warm, inviting atmosphere was filled with the soft hum of voices and the faint sound of jazz music playing in the background. They found a small booth by the window and settled in, each ordering a drink.

The waiter came by, bringing their drinks—an iced coffee for Shyamen, a latte for Earl, and hot chocolate for Eda. The warm, comforting aroma filled the air, blending with the soft jazz that played overhead.

"So, Eda," the girl said, taking a sip of her drink, "I think Earl mentioned you once. I remember him telling me about the time he accidentally splashed mud on a schoolgirl—was that you? I'm Shyamen, by the way—Earl's cousin and his 'good sister,' as he likes to call me." She extended her hand with a warm, friendly smile.

Eda shook her hand, throwing a teasing glance at Earl with a raised eyebrow. Yes, that innocent victim was me. And believe me, I made him work hard for forgiveness!

Earl leaned back with a smirk, chuckling lightly. She definitely taught me a valuable lesson about being a disciplined driver. Ha ha!

They laughed, and the tension Eda had felt earlier began to ease as the conversation flowed. Earl asked her about school, and soon, Shyamen chimed in, genuinely interested in Eda's stories about her school debates and sports events.

Earl leaned back with a playful grin. So, Eda, how's it going with you and your friends' savings accounts? Have you finally figured it all out? He teased, clearly in a good mood. Turning to Shyamen, he chuckled, these studious girls have been lecturing me on the importance of saving, just like their economics teacher taught them!

Eda turned to Shaymen, purposefully ignoring Earl's mocking comments. You know, Shaymen, she began, her tone slightly amused, 'some bankers who present themselves as high-profile professionals really lack the basics in marketing skills.

Shaymen looked puzzled, raising an eyebrow. 'What do you mean by that? She asked.

Well, she continued, a hint of sarcasm in her voice, when a customer walks in, they're not exactly welcomed. Instead, they're treated like troublemakers and just passed off to subordinates without a second thought.

Earl picked up on the hint she was dropping, smiling knowingly. Come on, Eda, he said gently, there's a certain protocol for these things. The officers who specialize in these matters are the ones who should handle them. It's our job to make sure things are delegated properly.'

Protocol, huh? Eda replied, her voice playfully challenging. But if a customer isn't satisfied after being handed off to a subordinate, they're going to feel undervalued, and that makes them less likely to want to make a deposit. Just think about it: if the customer feels respected and sees the officer going the extra mile, that $5,000 deposit could easily become $10,000—all because of a positive experience."

Earl chuckled, raising his hands in a mock surrender. Alright, alright, point taken. Thanks for the lesson, Eda. I'd say you've definitely given me an eye-opener.' He smiled warmly. 'Thanks for keeping us sharp!

Eda shrugged with a smile. What can I say? I believe in standing up for what's right—even if it means making a little noise."

The three of them laughed, enjoying the growing camaraderie as they shared stories and opinions. Eda felt herself relaxing more and more, grateful for Shyamen's easygoing warmth and Earl's unexpectedly attentive nature.

As their coffee break was coming to an end, Earl leaned forward, his expression gentle. "You know, Eda, you have a rare spirit. I really mean that."

Eda felt her cheeks get warm, but she smiled and said, "Well, someone has to keep things fun around here, right?"

Shaymen chuckled, catching onto the playful tension. You know, Earl, maybe you should just hire Eda as a trainee for your bank.

Earl laughed, shaking his head. "Not a bad idea! Only problem is...she's still underage," he teased, grinning at Eda.

Eda smiled, giving a little shrug. Guess I'll have to wait a bit longer then.

Alright," Earl said, standing up. Let's get moving. I'll drop you home, Eda.

Oh, don't bother, Earl," Eda replied quickly. Just drop me at the bus stop—it's no big deal.

Earl waved it off. No, no, it's not a problem. Come on, hop in.

Relenting, Eda climbed into the back seat, still smiling.

Chapter 10: The Evening Surprise

After a refreshing shower that evening, Eda slipped into bed with a book, trying to relax. But her mind kept replaying the morning's events, detail by detail. A soft smile tugged at her lips—she felt a quiet thrill, though she couldn't quite put her finger on why.

Just then, her phone buzzed loudly, breaking the silence. She squinted at the screen, curious about who would call at this hour. To her surprise, it was Earl's name flashing across the screen. Her heart skipped a beat as she quickly answered.

Hi, Eda. Are you free to talk?

Yes... I'm free, she replied, feeling a bit flustered.

Great to see you today, he said with a playful tone. But I'm curious—why did you suddenly go quiet after you called me?

Eda rolled her eyes, trying to sound calm. Well, I figured I'd thanked you enough already. Didn't want to overdo it, you know, she said, attempting to sound dignified.

Oh, I see, he chuckled. Alright, fair enough. By the way, do you know why I called?

No, she replied, curious now. Tell me.

Could you come to the bank tomorrow before 3 p.m.? Earl asked. But not in your school uniform. . Go home, change, and then come over.

Eda raised an eyebrow, intrigued. Why, are you planning some kind of grand welcome for me?

Not exactly, he laughed. I thought I'd set up a savings account for you.

Eda let out a soft, embarrassed laugh. Ah, Earl, that's sweet, but right now, I can't really ask my parents for money. They just paid for my brother's school enrollment.

Earl's voice turned light-hearted. Who said anything about asking for money? Just come, will you?

Also, please text me your accurate details right now, like your full name, age, NIC number, date of birth, home address, etc. And don't share this with your school friends—they might show up at the bank demanding savings accounts for themselves too! Ha ha!

Before she could reply, he added, Alright then, Eda. See you tomorrow around 2:30 p.m. Good night, and take care. The line went dead, leaving her with a racing heart and a smile she couldn't help but wear.

Eda pondered, wondering why he was so eager to help her. Was it because she had been honest and too open about her financial difficulties? She sighed, recognizing that her mom would likely understand, but her dad would probably be suspicious and might blame her for getting into this situation.

For now, she decided to keep this little secret to herself. A sense of calm enveloped her, making her feel lighter as she held onto this moment.

With a content smile, Eda nestled into her pillow and drifted off to sleep, her heart brimming with possibilities.

Scene at the Bank

At exactly 2:30 PM, Eda approached the bank entrance. The Security Officer greeted her and said, Mr. Earl Davidson asked me to direct you to his cubicle. He mentioned that he is expecting a customer at 2:30 PM.

Thanks! Eda replied, making her way into the cubicle.

Inside, Earl was seated with a warm smile, leaning toward the door. Hmm... you're right on time! Good quality, he teased, and Eda felt her cheeks flush.

Just a habit, she said, her usual confidence faltering slightly.

May I see your NIC? Earl requested, reaching for the intercom. Yes, sir, came a voice from the other end. Doreen, can you come for a moment? I need those forms for signatures.

Okay, sir, Doreen replied.

A moment later, Doreen arrived with a stack of forms. Earl directed her, Get Eda's signature in the necessary places. After Eda signed, Doreen took her NIC to make a copy and soon returned it, saying, I'll bring the savings book and ATM card in about 15 minutes.

Thanks, Doreen, Earl replied as she left.

Turning to Eda, he inquired, how are things? Why is your usual chatterbox so quiet today?

I'm saving energy for a big debate later!

Earl smiled and said, saving energy? Just don't fall asleep before the debate!

Earl ordered some refreshments, then turned serious. "Eda, I want you to know—don't think of this in a suspicious way. I genuinely feel that I need to offer a helping hand to someone as talented as you. With financial support, you can go a long way. But please, keep this between us. I don't want a crowd of your friends demanding savings accounts too.

They both laughed, the tension easing between them.

Moments later, Doreen returned with the savings book and ATM card, explaining how to activate the account. After she left, Eda opened the book, her eyes widening in disbelief. "Five thousand dollars?!

Its okay, Earl reassured her. You can use the money for your necessities. I'll ensure enough funds are deposited each month.

Tears welled in Eda's eyes as she spoke, I'm so sorry, Earl. I hurt you. I scolded you... how silly of me.

Please stop that nonsense, he said softly. If that incident hadn't occurred, I wouldn't have been able to offer this help to you. Your outburst was a wake-up call for me—it made me realize I needed to drive more carefully. And regarding your lengthy discussion on customer satisfaction at the café...

Ha! Right? Eda laughed, wiping her eyes.

As she got up to leave, she casually said, By the way, don't worry— I won't tell anyone.

Great. Just keep it to yourself, Earl replied with a smile as she walked out of the cubicle. They both felt a sense of relief, understanding that being open with each other had created a foundation for authentic support and a deeper friendship.

Chapter 11: of Wings of Ambition

Eda returned home feeling as light as a feather, her heart brimming with a whirlwind of emotions. The evening spent with Earl replayed in her mind like a beautiful dream—was it real?

After dinner, Eda settled into bed, clutching her bank book tightly. In the stillness of the night, she made a quiet promise to herself. Earl had such unshakable confidence in her, truly believing that one day she could make a mark in the world with her talents and capabilities. She vowed that she would never let him down. With a renewed sense of purpose, Eda resolved to make the most of his generous support, to channel it fully into reaching her dreams and showing him just how much his faith in her truly meant.

Still, there was one delicate hurdle she needed to overcome—her mother. Eda knew that any shift in her spending habits would be noticed immediately; her mom had a sharp eye for finances and seemed to have an instinctive awareness of every need or want Eda expressed. She could already picture her mom's concerned look if she suspected something unusual was going on.

Eda took a deep breath, deciding it was time for a diplomatic approach. The next afternoon, after school—when her mom was usually most relaxed—felt like the right moment to bring it up. She thought carefully, knowing this would be the best time to ease her mom into the idea.

Mom, can we talk for a minute? She asked, leaning against the counter.

Mom, Eda began, her voice steady yet soft, I wanted to tell you earlier but couldn't find the right moment." She hesitated just a bit, then continued, "Last Saturday, when I was picking out the books from the list you gave me, I ran into Earl. She paused, watching her mother's reaction before adding, "He was there with his cousin, Shaymen. They were so kind—they even invited me for a coffee and gave me a lift home afterward. We had such a lovely chat, and I actually learned a lot about them.

Her mother looked fascinated, that sounds nice, Eda.

Mom, remember how you said Earl is so kind and thoughtful?" Eda began, choosing her words with care. "Well, he actually suggested helping me financially and even recommended I open a bank account at his bank. That way, I can really focus on my studies and goals without any added stress. Her heart raced as she spoke, though she kept her tone steady. "It would mean I could use that support without putting any extra burden on you or Dad."

Her mother raised an eyebrow, clearly thinking it through. "A savings account?" she echoed. "That does sound helpful. But, Eda, are you certain this is a good idea? What does Earl expect in return?"

Eda quickly reassured her,"No, Mom, it's nothing like that at all. Earl truly believes in me and my talents—he just wants to help because he knows I could use the support. It's purely a kind gesture." She paused, then added carefully, but please, let's keep this between us for now. You know how Dad might react if he hears about a boy helping me financially. He'd likely jump to conclusions, and it would only make things more complicated.

Her mother studied her, sensing the earnestness in Eda's eyes. After a moment, she sighed, Alright, sweetheart. If this means that much to you, I won't say a word. But you need to be careful and keep me updated on how it goes."

Eda smiled, relief flooding her. Thank you, Mom. I promise to be responsible with every bit of it. I'll use Earl's support to sharpen my skills and make you both proud.

After a moment of contemplation, her mother nodded slowly. Alright, sweetheart. I trust you. Just remember to keep me updated on how things are going, okay?

Eda's heart swelled with gratitude. "Thank you, Mom! I promise to keep you informed and be responsible every step of the way. I won't let you, Dad, or Earl down."

After her mother's positive response, a wave of relief enveloped her. With her mom's support, Eda felt empowered to embrace this new chapter with newfound confidence, eager to transform Earl's encouragement into a stepping stone toward her dreams.

As Eda left the room, Gladys, Eda's mother, sat quietly, her mind swirling with thoughts. She understood that Henry, her husband, would always want the best for their daughter, but his protective nature often made him skeptical of anyone who might influence her, especially a boy like Earl. Henry had a wealth of life experience, which made him acutely aware of the complexities of the world outside their home.

It wasn't that he doubted Eda's ambitions or integrity; rather, he felt an instinctual need to shield her from potential harm. As a loving father, he was naturally inclined to be cautious about anyone who might enter Eda's life, particularly those who offered support. However, Gladys also recognized that Eda was no ordinary girl. Her daughter had a remarkable ability to navigate situations with wisdom and intuition. Gladys had always admired how Eda seemed to possess an innate sense of self-preservation, often guiding herself with an understanding that surpassed her years.

With a gentle sigh, Gladys reassured herself. She had faith in Eda's judgment and knew her daughter would not make foolish decisions. So, with a resolute heart, she decided to keep this information to herself for the time being, allowing Eda to seize this opportunity without the weight of her father's skepticism. After all, she thought, there would come a time when sharing this news would be appropriate—when Henry could appreciate the depth of Eda's commitment and the genuine intentions behind Earl's offer. Until then, she would hold onto this secret, trusting that everything would unfold as it should.

Chapter 12: Rising to the Challenge

Eda stood at the threshold of her future, the dim light of the library casting a warm glow around her determined expression. It was the night before the law entrance exam, and the air buzzed with a cocktail of excitement and anxiety. Eda had poured herself into her studies for weeks, her eyes tired but her spirit unyielding. The prestigious law school she had long admired was within reach, and she couldn't afford to falter now.

The room around her reflected her dedication: stacks of legal textbooks precariously piled on her desk, highlighted notes strewn across the floor, and her trusty laptop open to a document filled with meticulously crafted arguments. She leaned back in her chair, glancing at the clock—her heart raced as she realized it was already getting late.

Just then, she grabbed her phone, scrolling through her contacts until she found Earl's name. Her heart fluttered. Earl had been a guiding light in her life, a source of encouragement and wisdom, and tonight she needed that support more than ever.

As she dialed, the phone rang only once before Earl picked up. "Eda! How are you holding up?" His voice was warm and comforting, like a reassuring blanket on a cold night.

"Hey, Earl," she said, trying to keep her voice steady. "I'm feeling a bit... well, you know, anxious. Tomorrow is the big day."

"Of course it is!" Earl chuckled softly. "But let me remind you of something important. Remember, this is just one step in your journey, not the end of the world. You've worked too hard to let nerves get the best of you."

"I know," she replied, her voice trembling slightly. "But what if I mess up? What if I forget everything I studied?"

"Eda, stop right there," he said firmly, but kindly. "You've absorbed so much knowledge; it's all in there. Just trust yourself. You are more prepared than you think. It's like a race—stay focused on the finish line, not on the crowd."

She could almost picture Earl pacing back and forth in his living room, gesturing animatedly as he always did during their conversations. "You've got this! Imagine walking into that exam room, confidence radiating from you. Picture yourself answering those questions with clarity. Visualize it!"

Eda laughed softly, the tension in her shoulders easing. "You make it sound so easy! I wish I could have your confidence."

"Confidence isn't something you just have; it's something you build. Look at how far you've come! You didn't just decide to take this exam on a whim. You've been preparing for this moment for years." He paused, allowing his words to sink in. "And don't forget—you're not alone in this. I believe in you, and I'm proud of you."

"Thanks, Earl. That really means a lot to me," she said, feeling her resolve strengthen.

"Just remember," he continued, his tone shifting to a more serious note, "this exam doesn't define you. It's just one of many hurdles in life. No matter the outcome, I'll always support you."

Eda felt a swell of gratitude. "I really appreciate that. I promise I'll give it my all."

"Now, do you have everything ready? Your notes, your lucky pen?" he teased.

"Yes, and I'll make sure to get a good night's sleep," she replied, a hint of determination returning to her voice. "But I'll probably end up tossing and turning all night."

"Good plan! Just remember to breathe. And if you can't sleep, use that time to visualize your success again. I'll be here rooting for you, Eda. Call me after the exam, okay? I want to hear all about it."

"Definitely. Thanks again, Earl. You always know what to say to lift my spirits," she said, her heart lighter.

"Anytime, my girl. Now go wrap things up, and get some rest. Tomorrow's a big day, and I can't wait to celebrate your success!"

As Eda hung up the phone, she felt a newfound energy coursing through her veins. Earl's words echoed in her mind—words that reminded her of her strength and potential. She looked around her cluttered library, her sanctuary of knowledge, and took a deep breath, filled with a sense of purpose.

With renewed determination, she meticulously organized her notes one last time and set her alarm for the morning. She visualized walking into the exam room, exuding confidence and clarity. Tomorrow was the day she had worked tirelessly for, and she was ready to embrace it head-on. As she slipped under the covers, Eda allowed herself to dream of the future that awaited her, one where she could make her mark in the world of law, just as she had always envisioned.

The next morning dawned bright and clear, as if the universe itself was cheering her on. Eda arrived at the examination hall, her heart racing with a mixture of excitement and nerves. She spotted familiar faces—friends and fellow aspirants—but today, she felt a sense of purpose that set her apart from the rest. As the clock ticked down to the start of the exam, she closed her eyes for a moment, envisioning herself confidently tackling each question.

When the exam papers were distributed, Eda's nerves transformed into fierce determination. The questions were challenging, but with each one she answered, her confidence grew. She navigated through case studies and legal principles with a clarity that surprised even herself. Hours later, as she submitted her paper, a wave of relief washed over her. She had done her best, and now, all she could do was wait.

As soon as she stepped out of the examination hall, Eda pulled out her phone, her heart racing with the desire to share the moment with Earl. She dialed his number, feeling a rush of excitement. The call connected, but she was met with the sound of his voice echoing in a bustling background.

"Earl! It's Eda!" she exclaimed, her voice bubbling with enthusiasm.

"Eda! I'm in a meeting right now," he said, his tone warm yet slightly distracted. "How did it go?"

"I think I did well! The questions were tough, but I felt prepared. I really think I nailed it!" Eda's words flowed out, her joy palpable.

"That's fantastic!" Earl replied, his voice lighting up even amid the meeting chaos. "I knew you would. You've worked so hard for this moment."

"I can't wait to see the results! Thank you for all your support," Eda said, feeling a wave of gratitude wash over her.

"Remember, no matter the outcome, you've accomplished something amazing just by taking this step," he reminded her, his voice steady and reassuring. "I'm proud of you."

"I appreciate that," she said, her heart swelling with happiness. "I'll keep you updated once I hear back."

"Absolutely! And let me know when you're free to celebrate," he added, his excitement palpable even through the phone.

"Will do! I can't wait to tell you all about it," she said, her spirits soaring. After they exchanged a few more encouraging words, Eda hung up, a wide smile spreading across her face. The sun shone down brightly, and for the first time that day, she allowed herself to feel the weight of her accomplishment.

As she walked away from the exam hall, a sense of anticipation bubbled within her. The future was bright, and no matter what the results would be, she felt ready to embrace whatever came next.

Weeks passed, filled with anxious anticipation, until the day the results were finally announced. Eda woke up that morning with a jittery excitement fluttering in her stomach. "Today's the day! Today's the day!" she chanted to herself as she got ready, her usual energy radiating around her.

As she made her way down the stairs, she caught sight of her parents in the kitchen. Her mom, Gladys, was pouring a cup of coffee, while her dad, Henry, read the newspaper at the table. Eda paused for a moment, feeling a rush of gratitude for their unwavering support.

"Hey, superstar!" her dad called out, glancing up with a warm smile. "Are you ready for the big day?"

"I'm ready, Dad! I can't believe it's finally here!" Eda beamed, her nerves settling slightly with the sound of his encouraging voice.

"Just remember, no matter what happens, we're proud of you," her mom added, stepping over with a steaming cup of coffee. "You've worked so hard for this, Eda. Just go in there and show them what you've got!"

Eda's heart swelled with love. "Thanks, Mom! I'll make you proud!"

"Go knock them dead, kiddo!" Henry said, giving her an affectionate nudge as she reached for her backpack.

"Yeah, just remember to breathe and take your time," Gladys reminded her, brushing a strand of hair behind Eda's ear. "You've got this!"

With her parents' warm wishes and blessings echoing in her ears, Eda felt a wave of confidence wash over her. "I will! I'll call you the minute I find out!"

"Can't wait to hear the good news!" her dad called after her as she stepped outside, feeling ready to face the day.

With the sun shining brightly overhead and her family's love propelling her forward, Eda felt unstoppable as she headed to her laptop, her heart pounding in her chest like a drum.

Eda stepped onto the campus of law school, her heart racing with anticipation. She made her way to the notice board, where the list of successful candidates was posted. A crowd had gathered, their murmurs filled with a mix of excitement and anxiety. Eda pushed through, her eyes scanning the names, each heartbeat echoing louder in her ears.

Finally, she spotted it—her name! A wave of exhilaration washed over her as tears of joy sprang to her eyes. "I did it! I'm in!" she shouted, unable to contain her excitement. The people around her turned, smiles breaking out as they celebrated their own successes.

With a beaming smile, Eda pulled out her phone and quickly called Earl. "I did it! I'm officially a lawyer!"

"Of course you are! I always knew you would be," Earl replied, his voice filled with pride.

"I can't believe it! This is just the beginning!" Eda exclaimed, her excitement bubbling over.

"Remember, this journey is just as important as the destination. Keep that fire alive, Eda!"

"I will! I promise to make you proud!" Eda said, her heart swelling with joy as she envisioned the future ahead of her.

After hanging up, Eda dialed her parents. "Mom, Dad! I passed!

"That's amazing, sweetheart!" her mom exclaimed.

"We're so proud of you!" her dad added, his pride evident in his voice.

"I promise to make you both proud!" Eda said, her heart swelling with joy as she joined her fellow students in celebration.

Final Chapter: A Sunday Evening Reunion

It was a cozy Sunday evening, and Eda and Earl sat across from each other in their favorite café, enjoying a rare moment of calm. Even after a decade, whenever they were together, the world seemed to shrink, leaving them as playful as their younger selves.

Earl leaned back, grinning as he looked at Eda. So, Ms. Top Lawyer of the Year, he teased, tell me, what's it like having your name on every major case in the country? Must be exhausting being famous.

Eda laughed and rolled her eyes. Oh, please! We both know the real star here is the bank's chief executive—the golden boy of finance! Who would have guessed you'd not only pass those exams but actually run the whole place?

Earl raised an eyebrow. "All thanks to your endless lectures on planning, strategy, and—what was it?—'long-term vision'? You were right, though. You've always been the brains behind this operation."

Obviously!" Eda shot back with a smirk, giving him a playful nudge. "Without me, you'd still be tripping over fiscal policies and getting lost in finance reports.

Earl chuckled, a warm glint in his eyes. "Well, I just gave you a bit of perspective here and there, Ms. Chatterbox. The rest... that's all you."

Eda tilted her head, a soft smile spreading across her face as she acknowledged the truth. Fine, I admit it. You were always there when I needed someone steady—quietly nudging me in the right direction. She paused, her voice lowering with gratitude. If it weren't for you, I might not be sitting here as 'Ms. Top Lawyer.

Earl met her gaze, his expression tender. You've always had the fire, Eda. I was just lucky to be around to see it in action."

They both shared a laugh, the sound of it filling the cozy space around them, bringing them back to the old days.

Earl looked at her with a warm smile. You know, Eda, you'll always be that same passionate school girl I met—talkative, ambitious, and stubborn as ever.

Eda crossed her arms, pretending to pout. And you'll always be Mr. Mud Splash' to me. Remember when I nearly chased you down the street after that disaster?

Earl held up his hands in surrender. "How could I forget? The day I met a firestorm in school uniform."

Eda giggled, shaking her head. "Oh, and here we are ten years later, planning a wedding. Speaking of which...who should we invite?"

Earl leaned in, lowering his voice with a grin. "How about just close friends, family, and a few mentors? Maybe we should skip the high-profile crowd. Imagine how scandalized they'd be if they found out I was once called Mr. Mud Splash.

Eda stifled a laugh, nodding. And my juniors have to be there. They've been like family.

Earl nodded, a thoughtful expression on his face. That sounds like a solid plan. Let's keep it small and intimate. I want to be surrounded by those who've been there from the start—those who have witnessed our entire journey. He chuckled. And we can't forget your loyal school friends who came to open their bank accounts here! Ha ha!

Eda smirked. "What can I say? They know how to support a good cause! Her eyes softening as she met his gaze. It's been quite a journey, hasn't it? Ten years of... everything.

Earl, when I saw you and that girl Shayamen at the book stall, my heart nearly stopped. I thought she was your fiancée!" Eda confessed, her voice a mix of embarrassment and relief.

Earl threw his head back, laughing heartily. "You should've told me sooner! I would've had so much fun teasing you, he said with a playful nudge. So, did you actually get jealous?

Eda shot him a playful glare, crossing her arms. Mad? Are you kidding? My gut feeling was shouting, why are you even worried? Go up and talk to him. He's not your boyfriend. Show him you couldn't care less! And, well, that's just me."

Earl nodded, his smile softening as he watched her. Classic Eda, he said with a touch of admiration. Always confident, even in moments of doubt.

Of course, she replied, grinning. I'm not one to make a fuss.

Earl's smile grew, and he explained, "Shayami's actually my cousin. We're close friends too, but that's it. In fact, back in her college days, I was the one who helped her sneak letters to her boyfriend since her family was against the relationship.

Eda's eyes widened with interest. Really? Did she end up marrying him?

No, Earl chuckled. She married a doctor instead. Life took her in a different direction. He paused, his gaze thoughtful, as if recalling the memory. But, funny enough, after I dropped you home that night, she said something that surprised me.

Eda raised an eyebrow, intrigued. Oh? And what did she say? Earl leaned in, lowering his voice as if sharing a secret. She told me, Earl, give that girl some real thought. Don't let work consume you so much that you miss out on a personal life. She seems like an ideal partner for you. I could see how much you both enjoyed each other's company—your conversations were lively and engaging. I'm serious about this.

Eda's expression softened, a mixture of vulnerability and warmth in her eyes. She's a wise one, isn't she? You know, Earl, finding someone who truly understands me and let me be myself without judgment—it's rare, Eda said, her voice soft and filled with emotion. She gave him a gentle smile. May be that's why... seeing you with Shayami felt like losing something I wasn't ready to let go of.

Earl looked at her, a gentle smile in his eyes. Well, Eda, I'm here. I'm not going anywhere. Earl gently took her hand, his thumb gliding over her fingers. And to think it all began with a splash of muddy water. His eyes twinkled with affection. You're still that fiery chatterbox, Eda—just with a lot more courtroom victories now.

She beamed, lifting her chin with playful pride. I was always destined for greatness, all thanks to you and that endless 'wise vision' you kept preaching!

Earl's smile grew broader. "Indeed, I did have some pretty good ideas, didn't I? She laughed and leaned into him. Okay, I'll admit that. But I'm still the one with all the charm.

Earl shook his head, feigning a sigh. You've got a point there. I don't know anyone else who can talk as much as you and still make it engaging.

They laughed, their joy echoing through the café, harmonizing with the soft jazz playing in the background. After a moment, Earl held her gaze, his smile softening.

Eda, thank you. For everything. Eda looked back at him, her expression sincere and heartfelt. Earl, your belief in me has meant the world. You've always seen my potential, even when I didn't. That support has helped me shine.

Her smile softened as she gazed at him, and without saying a word, she squeezed his hand. The café felt peaceful around them, and in that moment, words were unnecessary. They both understood how far they had come together, their shared history culminating in this warm, beautiful moment.

The Heart of a Gentle Guide

Earl was not just any friend; he was a steadfast presence in Eda's life, a beacon of support who believed in her when she struggled to believe in herself. With a quiet strength, he watched her flourish from a girl with dreams too big for her modest means into a talented young woman ready to conquer the world. In those teenage years, when her parents could barely afford the basics, Earl stepped in with patience and understanding. He recognized the spark within her, the potential waiting to be ignited.

It was a thoughtful gesture that would change everything—opening a bank account for Eda. Each month, he deposited money, ensuring that she had the tools and resources to chase her ambitions. It wasn't merely a financial act; it was a lifeline. He wanted nothing in return, only to see her thrive. Earl understood the weight of her aspirations, the pressure of unmet expectations, and he was determined to ease her burden.

As time passed, something beautiful blossomed between them. What began as a pure desire to help turned into a deeper connection. Earl found himself captivated by Eda—not just by her talent, but by her spirit, her resilience, and her laughter. The magic of love crept in slowly, enveloping him in warmth as he realized that the girl he had once seen as a project had become the center of his world.

Earl's devotion was not loud or flashy; it was quiet and enduring, woven into the very fabric of their lives. He cherished every moment they shared, from late-night conversations about dreams to the simple joys of being in each other's company. He had nurtured her talents, but in the process, his heart had been touched in ways he never anticipated.

This was the essence of love—a blend of selflessness and recognition, where two paths merged into one. Earl was a testament to the idea that true devotion lies not just in grand gestures but in the small, everyday acts of kindness that create lasting bonds. Their story serves as a reminder that sometimes the most profound love is found in the gentle encouragement of another, and that nurturing someone else's dreams can lead to discovering your own heart's desire.

Ultimately, it wasn't just about helping Eda; it was about how supporting her allowed Earl to uncover the depths of his own love. In the process, they both grew into the best versions of themselves. The memories they created together would forever remain in their hearts, serving as a beautiful testament to the power of patience, understanding, and love.

The End